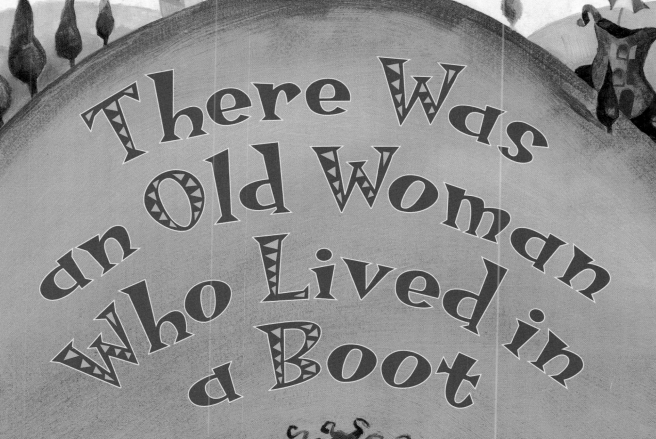

There Was an Old Woman Who Lived in a Boot

by
Linda Smith

Illustrated by
Jane Manning

HarperCollinsPublishers

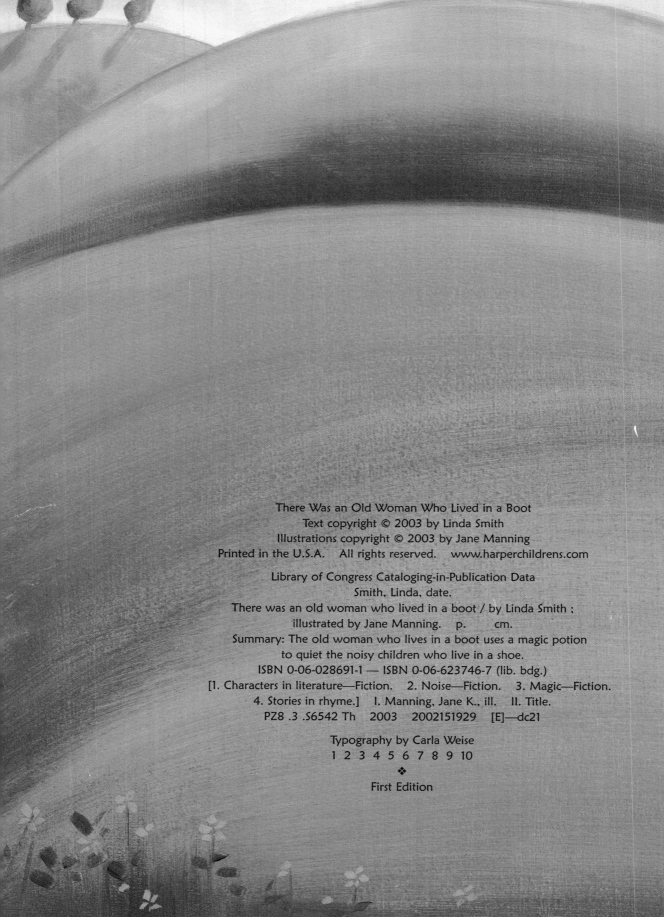

There Was an Old Woman Who Lived in a Boot

Text copyright © 2003 by Linda Smith

Illustrations copyright © 2003 by Jane Manning

Printed in the U.S.A.   All rights reserved.   www.harperchildrens.com

Library of Congress Cataloging-in-Publication Data

Smith, Linda, date.

There was an old woman who lived in a boot / by Linda Smith ;
illustrated by Jane Manning.   p.   cm.

Summary: The old woman who lives in a boot uses a magic potion
to quiet the noisy children who live in a shoe.

ISBN 0-06-028691-1 — ISBN 0-06-623746-7 (lib. bdg.)

[1. Characters in literature—Fiction.   2. Noise—Fiction.   3. Magic—Fiction.
4. Stories in rhyme.]   I. Manning, Jane K., ill.   II. Title.

PZ8 .3 .S6542 Th   2003   2002151929   [E]—dc21

Typography by Carla Weise

1 2 3 4 5 6 7 8 9 10

❖

First Edition

To my neatest, sweetest, greatest,
top-ratest friends, Karma Wilson,
Lisa Wheeler, my husband Russ,
and all my rumble-down,
tumble-down Hendershott
children who inspired this book
—L.S.

For Poppy.
I love you and miss you
—J.M.

There was an old woman who didn't like children,
Who lived in a musty old, crusty old boot,
Who had an old cat who didn't like kittens,
Who didn't like *anything* little or cute.

Then along came another, a remarkable mother!
Who moved into a rumble-down, tumble-down shoe,
Who shattered the quiet,
Who caused quite a riot,
With her clattering, chattering, clamoring crew!

NOW what would the old woman do?

She peeked through the laces, spied all those cute faces,
Then turned to the cat in a horrible mood.
"The nerve of that crowd! So noisy! So loud!"
The cat quite agreed they were terribly rude.

As it happened that day, the old witch down the way
Had a sale on old lotions and potions and such.
And there on her lawn was some "KIDDIE-BE-GONE"—
A bit stale (but it didn't cost much).

The witch said, "My dear, the instructions are clear.
You must follow them right to the letter."
But if a teaspoon or two would sufficiently do,
The old woman thought *ten* would work better.

So she and the cat dumped it all in a vat,
Setting sweet little chairs in the shade.
They even made ice! Now wasn't that nice?
And a sign that said "Free Lemonade"!

The kiddies were grand, they came running as planned.
The old woman was trying her best.

Sounding oh so sincere, she said, "Welcome my dear,"
As she greeted and seated each guest.

Cup after cup the kiddies drank up,
Then fell to the ground in a heap.

The old woman was smirking. "My potion is working!
Each one of those pests is asleep!"

Each jibbering, jabbering lemonade drinker,
Each chittering, chattering wee little stinker,
Each squeaker, each squawker, each tittering talker,
Not one of the guests made a peep.

The old woman said, "Cat, we took care of that!"
With a cheer and a flick of the tail,
They cried, "Kiddies-Be-Gone!" (but did someone just yawn?)
They'd forgotten the potion was stale!

With a weak little wizzle, the magic went fizzle!
The heap stumbled and rumbled and rolled.
They weren't cute little kiddies—
They were grouches and biddies!
All rusty and crusty and old!

Some saggy and baggy, with moles on their skin,
Some crinkled and wrinkled, with rolls on their chin,
Some bumpy and lumpy,
Some terribly grumpy,
All musty and dusty with mold.

If that wasn't enough, they were grouchy and gruff—
They bellowed for supper and tea.
The old woman wailed,
"My potion has failed!
It's a curse! They are far worse than me!"

The sun was too bright, their tea wasn't right,
Either too sweet or not sweet enough.
They demanded a plate,
They complained as they ate,
That the roast was entirely too tough.

The cat made them wheeze
(they were sure she had fleas)—
Just the naggiest, craggiest crew.
They groused and they grumbled,
They rumbled and mumbled.

NOW what would the old woman do?

As it happened that day, the old witch down the way
Was unloading a box from her truck.
And there, a whole stack of "KIDDIE-COME-BACK"!
My goodness—imagine the luck!

The witch made a deal—the price was a steal,
And the potion was all guaranteed.
The old woman cried, "Great! I'll buy the whole crate!
What a bargain! It's just what I need!"

So she and the cat mixed it all in a vat,
But just as they served the old bunch—
Oh, what a commotion!
The cat slipped in the potion!
And fell whiskers and all in the punch!

The grouches and biddies shrank back into kiddies,
But where was the cat who fell in?
The old witch's spell made that cat shrink as well!
She turned into a kitten again!

There was an old woman who lived in a boot,
Who had an old cat who turned little and cute,
Who played with the children, who lived in the shoe,
The whole clattering, chattering, clamoring crew!

NOW what could that old woman do?

And from there ever after...
A RIOT OF LAUGHTER!